IN THE AMAZING BRAIN-TWISTER

BIG IDEA BOOKS

www.bigidea.com

Zonder**kidz**™

The children's group of Zondervan
www.zonderkidz.com

Larryboy in the Amazing Brain-Twister
Copyright © 2004 by Big Idea Productions, Inc.

Requests for information should be addressed to:
Zonderkidz, Grand Rapids, Michigan 49530

ISBN: 0-310-70651-3

Written by: Doug Peterson
Editors: Cindy Kenney and Amy DeVries
Cover and Interior Illustrations: Michael Moore
Cover Design and Art Direction: Paul Conrad, Karen Poth
Interior Design: Holli Leegwater, John Trent, and Karen Poth

CIP applied for
Printed in United States

04 05 06/RRD/5 4 3 2 1

LARRYBOY™
IN THE AMAZING BRAIN-TWISTER

WRITTEN BY
DOUG PETERSON

ILLUSTRATED BY
MICHAEL MOORE

BASED ON THE HIT VIDEO SERIES: LARRYBOY
CREATED BY PHIL VISCHER
SERIES ADAPTED BY TOM BANCROFT

Zonderkidz

TABLE OF CONTENTS

CHAPTER 1

TORNADO ALLEY
5:15 A.M.

There was something
strange in the air in Bumblyburg.
Black, ragged clouds hung low over the
city. The air had a greenish glow to it.
Thunder rumbled across the sky. It was still
very early on a Monday morning, so the streets
of Bumblyburg were almost empty. In fact, only a
single car moved through the downtown area.
Behind the wheel of that car was Officer Olaf, mak-
ing his rounds.

"Somewhere…over the rainbow—"sang Officer Olaf
in his heavy Swedish accent. He loved to belt out
songs while listening to his favorite radio show—*The
Accordion Hit Parade,* doncha know?

Perhaps if the radio had been turned down lower,
he might have realized that something strange and
sinister was racing up from behind.

A tornado!

Pulling up to a red stoplight, Olaf continued to
cut loose in song. "We represent the lollipop kids!
The lollipop kids…!"

If the kindly policeman had just looked

into his rearview mirror, he would have seen the swirling mass of black, twisting clouds slip up behind him. It was probably the only tornado in history to ever stop at a red light.

When the light turned green, Olaf finally took a quick look into his rearview mirror.

"AHHHHHHHHHHHHHH!" Officer Olaf made a screeching left turn. He was sure the tornado would continue to move straight. But here's the strange part…

The tornado made a sharp left turn, too.

Officer Olaf made a right turn.

The tornado made a right turn.

Officer Olaf increased his speed by twenty miles per hour.

So did the tornado.

Left turn, right turn, left turn!

He even made a complete turnaround and caused his squad car to flip up on two wheels, causing sparks to fly. But everything that Officer Olaf tried—failed. He couldn't shake this maniac monster of a tornado. It had to be the strangest car chase ever.

Officer Olaf suddenly remembered the old safety rule: never try to outrun a tornado in your car. So he brought his squad car to a screeching halt and tried to flee on foot—or whatever it is that vegetables flee on.

"Open up! Open up!" Olaf pounded on the door to the Shave and Shine Barber Shop. He needed to find a storm cellar fast! But the shop wasn't open yet. Olaf sprinted up Bumbly Boulevard, made a quick right turn, and found himself trapped in an alley—a dead-end alley. His heart sank as he stared up at the large brick wall in front of him.

The tornado turned into the alley, moving slowly toward him—like a monster that knew its victim was trapped.

CHAPTER 2

TWISTER!

6:45 A.M.

Meanwhile, in another part of Bumblyburg...
Larry the Cucumber loved rainy days and
Mondays. Why else would he get up extra early
just to play games before work?

"Left hand red, right hand green," said Archie, after
twirling a spinner. Archie was Larry's trusted butler.

Larry stood on a plastic mat, which was covered
with colored circles. He and Archie were beginning to
play the classic game Twister. But something didn't
seem quite right.

"What did you just say, Archie?" Larry asked.

"The spinner says to put your left hand on red,
your right hand on green."

Larry blinked a few times. He looked down at his
sides. "This isn't working, Archie."

But there was no time to think about that now.
A spotlight shot into the air, placing the
Larryboy emblem high in the dark, stormy sky.
And that meant only one thing. There was
trouble in Bumblyburg.

"I still say that a pager
would be an

easier way to reach me," said Larry, as Archie dialed the phone to find out what was wrong in the city.

"There's a robbery in progress at Mr. Snappy's Extremely Gigantic Toy Emporium," Archie exclaimed, hanging up the phone. "Quick! Not a moment to lose!"

Faster than lightning, Larry threw on his Larryboy costume, flossed his teeth with Larryfloss, slid down the Larrypole, leaped into the Larrymobile, clicked on his Larryseatbelts, and made sure his Larrymug was secure in the cup holder.

The Larrymobile raced out into the storm.

With weather-warning sirens blaring, the streets of Bumblyburg were still deserted. The only sign of life was at Mr. Snappy's Extremely Gigantic Toy Emporium, where an armored car was parked.

Larryboy leaped out of the Larrymobile and pushed his keyless-entry remote control. "Excuse me, Larryboy. But you've just set the car to self-destruct in ten minutes," the car computer told him. (Archie had equipped the Larrymobile with a computer that could talk. Larryboy called the computer Fred.)

"Peanut brittle," said Larryboy. "Thanks for the warning, Fred." Our plunger-headed hero pushed another button on his keyless remote and the Larrymobile was instantly transformed into a boat.

"Wrong button again," said Fred. "Or were you planning a moonlit cruise down Main Street?"

"Sarcasm from a computer?" Larryboy asked.

"The wonders of technology," Fred added.

After Larryboy finally pressed the correct button, the

Larrymobile switched back into a car and all of the locks clicked into place.

"Have a nice day. Be home by lunchtime," Fred told him as Larryboy bounded off.

It didn't take long for our hero to figure out what the trouble was. Somebody was stealing stuffed animals from the toy store and loading them into the armored car.

"Halt, toy napper!" declared Larryboy, as he jumped onto the roof of the armored car and struck a dramatic pose.

"Is that you, Larryboy?" came a voice from inside the armored car. Officer Olaf leaped out the side door.

"Officer Olaf?"

"Ya, it's true. You betcha, it's me," he said with a kindly twinkle in his eye.

Larryboy gave Olaf a puzzled look. "Your voice sounds a little deeper than usual."

"Just a cold," said Olaf. "It's going around, doncha know?"

Larryboy peered into the armored car, which was half-packed with stuffed animals.

"I don't understand," Larryboy observed. "Why all the toys?"

"Oh, it's really quite simple. We've been tipped off that a master criminal is going to try to steal stuffed animals from the toy store this very day. So I'm putting them into the armored car for safekeeping."

"Good idea!" Larryboy glanced back at the store, where piles of stuffed animals were waiting to be loaded into the car—like animals about to enter the ark. "Here, let me help you!"

"Much obliged, Larryboy."

For the next ten minutes, our superhero helped the policeman load up the car. "Another good deed done," said Larryboy, feeling pleased with himself as the armored car raced away.

Unfortunately, Larryboy didn't take a good, hard look at the license plate on that armored car. If he had, maybe he would have realized that something wasn't quite right about Officer Olaf—besides his strange voice.

The license plate read FOUL PLAY.

CHAPTER 3

OLAFS ALL OVER THE PLACE

7:23 A.M.

Larryboy
began the drive back to the
Larrycave. But as he pulled away from
the toy store, he accidentally pushed the
back-seat-driver button on Fred the Computer.
"You're driving too fast!" screeched Fred.
"Watch out for that fire hydrant! Slow down! Put
on your Larryblinker! How about some air conditioning back here?"

It took a few minutes, but a frantic Larryboy
finally figured out how to switch Fred back to normal.
Even Fred seemed relieved.

"Don't ever do that to me again," Fred scolded.
"And while you're at it, Larryboy, I'd swing by the
Bumblyburg police station."

"Why?"

"There's trouble with a capital *T*. And that rhymes
with *P*. And that stands for police station."

"What kind of trouble?" asked Larryboy.

"Don't ask me. I'm a computer, not a genius."

Turning his car around, Larryboy drove
straight for the police station.

Fred was right. Something definitely was going on. Several burly policemen were dragging a plum out of the station, but he wasn't going quietly.

"I may look like a plum, but I'm *Officer Olaf*, I tell you! I *work* here!" the plum shouted. "Take your hands off me!"

The policemen gave each other knowing glances. This plum was clearly off his rocker.

The plum claimed to be Officer Olaf and even sounded like the Swedish policeman, but he sure didn't look like Olaf. He was dressed like a scientist. He wore a white lab coat, complete with a pocket protector for his pens, and huge, thick, black-rimmed glasses. On the glasses were all sorts of blinking lights and gadgets. And mounted on his head was something that could only be described as a high-tech football helmet. Wires and lights covered the helmet like electronic ivy, and the whole lot of it was connected to a tiny radar dish sticking out of the top of it.

The plum spotted Larryboy, broke loose from the policemen, and ran up to the superhero.

"Larryboy, you've got to help me, doncha know?" the plum begged. "I'm Officer Olaf, but somehow my body has been changed into this...this...*plum!*"

"You can't be Officer Olaf," said Larryboy. "I just saw him a few minutes ago."

"Don't I sound like Olaf?"

"You're a good impersonator. Can you do the president?"

"Okay, I'll *prove* that I'm Officer Olaf!" the plum told Larryboy. "I'll tell you something that only you and I could know!"

But the plum never got a chance to prove himself. At

that very moment, a twister came roaring around the cor-
ner, hungry for destruction. It sucked up cars and spit out
the engines like prune pits. It shattered windows and
uprooted trees.

And in its path was the Larrymobile...

Sensing danger, Fred the Computer started the engine
and squealed out of the parking space—without anyone
behind the steering wheel.

"Hey, wait for me!" Larryboy shouted, running after his
car, which clearly had a mind of its own.

But so did the tornado. It knew exactly where it was
going as it swirled straight for the plum. Larryboy
watched in horror as the tornado bore down on the poor
plum, sucked him into the wild whirlwind, and then tore
off down the street.

CHAPTER 4

IF I ONLY HAD A HEART...

7:45 A.M

Larryboy
leaped into the Larrymobile.
"Follow that twister!" Larryboy yelled,
as he put the car into gear. But the
Larrymobile's engine sputtered and stalled.
"We're out of gas," said Fred. "Peanut
brittle! I was really looking forward to chasing
that tornado."
"We can't be out of gas!" Larryboy shouted.
"Archie filled the tank this morning."
"And look! The engine is overheated," said Fred.
Steam billowed from under the hood of the Larrymobile.
"I know what you're doing, Fred! You're trying to
get out of chasing that tornado!"
"Now why would I want to avoid chasing a storm
that is the most dangerous kind in nature? Whoops! Is
that a tire I hear falling off?"
One of the plunger tires on the Larrymobile
popped off and wobbled down the street.
In frustration, Larryboy clunked his head down
on the steering wheel, causing an air bag to dis-
charge in his face.

"Oops," said Fred. "My mistake."

Meanwhile, the terrifying twister roared through Bumblyburg, passed Bumbly Park, and left the city. It was headed straight for a tiny farmhouse in the middle of nowhere. But instead of flattening the house, it stopped on a spot right next to the barn. The ground opened up below the twister and the storm disappeared into the earth.

The twister dropped into a large, underground room and shut down its power. The black, twisting cloud vanished like a genie in a bottle. All that was left was a small, round vehicle, which had been spinning at the very center of the tornado. As it slowly came to a stop, a hatch popped open with a *hisssssss*.

Out stepped a plum...the very same plum who had been sucked up by the tornado just moments before. But this was no ordinary plum. He was diabolical. He was sinister. He was—

"Now wasn't that a funsy-wunsy ride?" the plum asked his Teddy Bear.

He was a plum that liked stuffed animals. But that didn't make him warm and fuzzy. *No sir!* This was one mean, old plum. His name: Plum Loco.

"Those fools have no idea that I switched brains with Officer Olaf and put my brain in his body," Plum Loco giggled to his Teddy Bear, one of a hundred stuffed animals cluttering up his secret laboratory. "And it was so *easy!* What a perfect way to steal stuffed animals!"

It was true. Plum Loco had used his twisted twister machine to switch brains with Officer Olaf. Plum Loco's brain wound up inside Officer Olaf's body, while Olaf's brain wound up in the plum's body. After pulling off the toy-store robbery, Plum Loco had reversed the process.

Their brains were back to normal—although Plum Loco wasn't someone who could really be referred to as normal.

On the wall in front of this plum was the giant map of a brain, spread out like a huge map of the world. The Veggie brain *was* Plum Loco's world. He was a brain surgeon gone bad.

Plum Loco thrived on being mean to others. He didn't have a heart, and he didn't care. In fact, he was sick of hearts. On Valentine's Day, he bought his chocolates in a brain-shaped box, rather than a heart-shaped box. His bumper sticker said, "Brains R Us."

He had even changed the titles of famous songs to:

"I Left My Brain in San Francisco."

"Put a Little Love in Your Brain."

"Achy Breaky Brain."

Plum Loco laughed, "Switching brains with Officer Olaf was only the beginning of Operation Unkind. I've got many more stuffed animals to pilfer and lots more Veggies to pick on. The question is, who's next?"

Plum Loco bent down and whispered into the ear of his Teddy Bear. "Perhaps I'll even switch brains with a superhero."

This guy had one twisted mind.

CHAPTER 5

TOO COOL FOR KINDNESS
10:30 A.M.

Tornadoes weren't the only force of nature in Bumblyburg.

At the *Daily Bumble* newspaper, other powers were on the loose. Their names were Ziggy Pickle and Ricky Avocado—two paperboys who thought they were too cool for words. Ziggy and Ricky were strong, good-looking, and popular. But they were also as unpredictable as twisters. Kindness was not their trademark.

Junior Asparagus, cub reporter for the *Daily Bumble*, tried to stay out of their way. Little did Junior know that, by some strange twist of fortune, today their paths would cross in a most unusual way.

It all started with stares. As Junior moved through the halls of the *Daily Bumble*, people kept turning and looking at him with puzzled expressions. And when he strolled by the circulation department, several paperboys and papergirls laughed and pointed. In fact, about the only papergirl who didn't snicker was his friend, Laura.

"Hey Junior!" called Laura Carrot, hopping up to him.

"What's with the hanger?"

"The what?"

"The clothes hanger," chuckled Laura. "There's a hanger sticking out the back of your shirt."

Junior craned his neck around. Sure enough, a clothes hanger was sticking out of his shirt. How humiliating! No wonder everyone was staring!

"I dressed kinda fast this morning and forgot to take it out," Junior said, blushing.

Junior decided he had better pull out the hanger as fast as he could, before anyone else saw him. But something made him pause. Two shadows passed over him like storm clouds. Slowly, he looked up and found himself staring into the dark eyes of Ziggy and Ricky.

His heart sank. This had to be the worst possible timing. Ziggy and Ricky were going to tease him for the rest of the year for showing up with a clothes hanger in his shirt. Junior felt like crawling into a hole.

But that didn't happen. Ziggy and Ricky stared at Junior for the longest, most awful minute. Finally, they spoke.

"Hey, that's actually pretty cool, Junior," said Ziggy.

"That's *way* cool," added Ricky. "Did you come up with the idea yourself?"

"Well...uh...Actually, I did."

Wow! Junior thought. *Do these guys really mean it? Do they actually think I'm cool because I'm wearing a clothes hanger in my shirt?*

"That's the coolest idea I've seen all year!" Ziggy beamed, stepping up beside Junior.

And then they spoke the words he never thought he would here...

"Hey, Junior, want to help us with our paper route today?"

Helping them deliver papers was one of the highest honors around. But Junior played it cool and tried not to look too excited.

"Sure, why not," he answered, jumping up and down and screaming for joy inside.

Laura wasn't nearly as excited. She didn't like the sound of this. It was as if warning sirens were going off in her brain like the ones alerting all of Bumblyburg to the stormy weather.

CHAPTER 6

BRAINSTORMS

11:00 A.M.

"It's a new style. I'm starting a fad," Junior told Larry the Janitor, as he entered the meeting room of the *Daily Bumble*. The clothes hanger was still sticking out of the back of his shirt.

"No kidding," said Larry. "That's pretty cool. Where can I get one of those?"

"Try a closet. They're called hangers," said Bob the Tomato, carrying a stack of papers into the room for the daily staff meeting.

"It's very bold," Larry said. "It really makes a statement."

"I'll give you a statement," Bob scowled. "Get back to work."

"Right away, Chief!" Larry said, as he hopped to it.

Larry the Janitor dusted in the background, while the staff talked news. It was their daily brainstorming session.

Little did the staff know that Larry, the mild-mannered janitor, was also the caped cucumber. He was the purple, plunger-headed defender of all that is good, true, and in need of vacuuming. He was...*Larryboy!*

"All right," said Bob, the top tomato at the newspaper. "What do we have for the front page, besides two stories on the tornadoes?"

"Plum Loco, the famous brain surgeon, is in town giving a lecture," said Vicki Cucumber, flipping through her notes.

"Sounds interesting," said Larry, dusting Bob's head.

"Larry, my head does *not* need dusting!" Bob shouted.

"Sorry." Larry started dusting Bob's coffee mug.

"We're trying to have a meeting here," said Bob. "Why don't you forget the dusting for now?"

"Sure thing, Chief."

Larry pulled out his vacuum cleaner—his trusty Cyclone 1000.

"So what do we have on the robbery at Mr. Snappy's Extremely Gigantic Toy Emporium?" asked Bob. "I heard that all of the stuffed animals were stolen."

Larry's heart leaped into his throat. (Not literally. That would be too gross. It's just an expression.) He was shocked.

"All of the stuffed animals were stolen?" Larry said. "Then Officer Olaf was right!"

"What do you mean?" asked Vicki.

"A friend of mine saw Officer Olaf putting stuffed animals into an armored car for protection this morning," said Larry. "Somebody must have stolen them from the armored car!"

But Mr. Snappy said the toys were stolen right out of his store," Bob clarified, very surprised. "He didn't say anything about giving them to Officer Olaf to protect!"

Larry turned on his vacuum cleaner and began to push it around the room.

"Vicki, you'd better check on this story about Officer

Olaf," Bob shouted over the noise of the vaccuum. "And turn that thing off, Larry! We're trying to talk!"

"Sure thing, Chief."

Unfortunately, Larry didn't push the Off button. By mistake, he pushed the button for supersuction cyclone.

ROOOOAAAARRRRRR!

The supersuction vacuum came alive and sucked up the drapes that Larry had been vacuuming. **THOOOOOMP!**

It was like a wild animal, devouring things right and left. **"LARRY, TURN THAT THING OFF!"**

"I'M TRYING!"

But it was too late. The Cyclone 1000 vacuum cleaner went on a rampage.

It sucked up all of Bob's papers from the table.

It swallowed an entire mug of coffee.

It chased two reporters around the conference table.

It sucked all of the water out of the water cooler.

It even latched onto Bob's nose.

In fact, the Cyclone 1000 might have swallowed Bob the Tomato whole if Larry hadn't finally remembered another way to stop the machine—he pulled out the plug.

Silence fell over the staff. The meeting room was in shambles.

"The commercial was right. This vacuum sure has supersuction power," said Larry.

At that moment, a piece of the ceiling crumbled and fell right on top of Bob. Larry hurried over and dusted the debris off of Bob's head.

"I guess you needed dusting after all," Larry said.

Bob wasn't smiling.

CHAPTER 7

AN EMERGENCY WEATHER BULLETIN
11:32 A.M.

We interrupt this story with an emergency weather bulletin.

A cool front has been seen moving through the halls of the *Daily Bumble* newspaper. This cool front, made up of several cool kids, is expected to move in from the west. The cool kids are heading toward warm, kind-hearted kids, creating a dangerous, unstable situation.

If you are anywhere near these cool kids, please find shelter immediately. We repeat. Please find shelter immediately.

We now return you to your regularly scheduled story...

CHAPTER 8

BULLY BOWLING

11:33 A.M.

Junior Asparagus strutted through the halls of the *Daily Bumble*, with Ricky on one side and Ziggy on the other. He felt like a king. Ricky and Ziggy were wearing hangers in their shirts, too.

A new style had been born.

The old disco song, "Staying Aloof," blared with every step they took. (Ziggy and Ricky always played that song on a boom box whenever they strutted down the hall.)

"OOO-OOO-OOO-OOO, STAYING ALOOF, STAYING ALOOF. OOO-OOO-OOO-OOO, STAYING ALOOOOOOF!" The three sang at the top of their lungs.

Paperboys and girls stared at them every step of the way. Only this time there were no snickers. If Ricky and Ziggy wore hangers, it *had* to be cool.

The trio made quite a team—Ziggy, Ricky, and Junior.

"Oh my," cooed a papergirl as they passed by and looked her direction.

Things were going great for Junior—until the triumphant trio came upon two of Junior's friends. Wally and Herbert were paperboys too and definitely *not* cool in the eyes of Ziggy and Ricky.

"Hey, let's have some fun," snickered Ziggy.

"I'm up for it," Ricky agreed.

"Let's not," squeaked Junior, but the two bullies weren't listening.

"Time to go bowling," Ziggy said.

Just what Junior was afraid of. You see, Ziggy and Ricky liked to bowl. But not the kind of bowling you're thinking of. When Ziggy and Ricky went bowling, they bowled Veggies over. They sent bowling balls zipping down hallways and sidewalks, knocking over broccoli, zucchinis, and carrots like bowling pins. You might say they were equal opportunity bowlers, and literally no one who got in the way stood a chance.

"I'm not really in the mood for bowling. What about soccer?" Junior asked, as Ziggy pulled his bowling ball out of his backpack. Ziggy never went anywhere without it.

"Nah, soccer's no fun."

"Then how about if we go get our paychecks?" Junior suggested.

"My money's not going anywhere," Ziggy said, lining up his shot.

Taking three bounces forward, Ziggy let loose. The bowling ball zoomed down the hall. His precision was amazing. Ziggy's ball hit Wally, knocking him into Herbert, and both of them crashed to the floor.

"Great shot!" shouted Ricky.

Herbert glanced up, his goofy sunglasses shattered. "Oh hi, Junior," he said, with a weak smile. "Nice hanger."

Junior didn't know what to say.

But he did know what to do. Junior knew God would want him to be kind. He knew he should help Wally and Herbert get back up. But if he did that, Ricky and Ziggy would turn on *him*.

"Are you friends with these two guys?" Ziggy asked Junior with a scowl.

Junior looked at Wally. Then at Herbert. Then he stared into the accusing eyes of Ziggy and Ricky.

"Ahh, not really," Junior said quietly.

"Good answer," Ziggy told him.

The trio continued to strut through the circulation department like kings...but Junior no longer felt like a king. A traitor was more like it.

"000-000-000-000, STAYING ALOOF, STAYING ALOOF! 000-000-000-000, STAYING ALOOOOOOF!"

CHAPTER 9

THE MASKED TAILOR!
12:01 P.M.

Meanwhile,
our plunger-headed hero headed to his Superhero 101 class, which
was usually held at the Bumblyburg
Community College.

But today was special. Their teacher, Bok
Choy, took them on a field trip to the Masked-
Tailor Superhero Costume Factory, secretly hidden
deep below an ordinary clothes store.

Most members of the superhero class were there—
Lemon Twist, Iron Clad, Electro-Melon, Bubble Gum,
Scarlet Tomato, and others. All of these heroes had
their costumes made at the factory. But the factory had
never been set up for superhero tours...until now.

"I am the Masked Tailor. Welcome to our factory,"
said the owner, a masked string bean dressed in
black. He wore the latest in capes—a high-tech cloak
that could even flap indoors without wind.

The tour was amazing. Bok Choy's superhero
class got to see where the Superseamstresses (all
wearing masks) sewed the costumes. They wandered through a museum that told the longtime
history of superhero costumes. (The very first

39

costumes were made out of rock, which explained why prehistoric superheroes couldn't fly more than a foot off the ground.)

After the "Salute to Spandex" musical show in the factory auditorium, the superheroes even got a chance to improve their costume-changing skills. A special simulation center had been set up with hundreds of telephone booths. Each superhero was timed on how fast he or she could change into their costumes and then emerge from the phone booths.

The class concluded in what looked like an ordinary classroom.

"I'd like to end this field trip with a one-question, extra-credit quiz," announced Bok Choy. "My question is this: what is the most important thing that a superhero should wear?"

The superheroes gave the usual answers: mask, cape, utility belt, emblem, magnetic undershirt, atomic-powered slippers.

But they were all wrong.

"For the answer, turn to Section 51, Paragraph 3, Line 12 in your *Superhero Handbook*," said Bok Choy.

The Scarlet Tomato read it aloud: "You are God's chosen people. You are holy and dearly loved. So put on tender mercy and kindness as if they were your clothes."

"None of our superpowers or supercostumes would be any good if we didn't clothe ourselves with kindness," said Bok Choy. "That way, when people look at us, they see our kindness—just as clearly as they see our superhero costumes. Remember: superheroes have a heart."

No sooner had he said this than the lights in the classroom began to flicker. Weather-warning sirens began
wailing. The Masked Tailor threw open the door and
shouted, "A twister is heading straight for the store
upstairs! You've got to help!"

The superheroes reacted with blazing speed.
Scrambling out of the room, they barged up a spiral stair-
case that led directly to the Vegetable Bin clothing store
above. What the superheroes saw was truly shocking.

Whirling right in front of the store was another tornado. But strangely enough, the twister simply spun in
place—like some giant, deadly top.

"Let me handle this!" Lemon Twist shouted. "This job
is right up my alley."

Right up her tornado alley, that is. Lemon Twist had
the amazing ability to control wind within a one-foot
radius of her body. She was the perfect match for the
twister roaring outside the door.

Lemon Twist went whirling outside. And that's when
the twister made its move. It rushed forward like a pounc-
ing beast. When the twister smashed into Lemon Twist,
the force of wind increased seven times over.

The roof of the clothing store ripped right off the top of
it. Hundreds of clothing items went flying out of the top of
the building like birds. The twister swallowed up Lemon
Twist, and then it turned and whirled away, leaving may-
hem in its trail.

CHAPTER 10

THE HEART OF DARKNESS
2:03 P.M.

The famous brain surgeon Plum Loco once again showed up at the police station. Only this time he claimed to be the superhero Lemon Twist. Stranger yet, the real Lemon Twist was spotted on the east side of town STEALING STUFFED ANIMALS out of the homes of Veggie children!

Larryboy was stunned.

"I can't believe that Lemon Twist would rob anyone," he told Archie back at the Larrycave.

"It's certainly odd," agreed Archie. "But here's something even stranger. The tornadoes cropping up around Bumblyburg don't appear to be naturally occurring. I think that they may have been artificially created by something evil."

Larryboy took a big gulp of his chocolate malt, leaving a chocolate mustache on his upper lip.

"If that's the case, then we should be able to turn these twisters off! But how?"

"There's only one way to find out."

"And what's that?" asked Larryboy.

Archie paused dramatically. "Someone must get into the very center of this mysterious whirlwind by flying into the tornado."

"Wow! But who would be crazy enough to fly into the middle of a twister?" Larryboy asked.

Archie continued to stare at Larryboy, as if to answer his question.

Larryboy glanced behind himself, hoping somebody else was standing there. There wasn't.

"Peanut brittle," said Larryboy. "You're looking at me, aren't you?"

Fifteen minutes later, he was soaring high over Bumblyburg in the Larryplane.

"This is crazy!" Larryboy said.

The caped cucumber couldn't believe that Archie had talked him into flying his plane right into a swirling mass of killer wind. He also couldn't believe the other problem that he had to deal with—Fred the Computer.

"Land this plane! **PLEEEEEEEEASE!**" pleaded Fred. "I'm afraid of heights!"

"You're a computer, Fred. How can you be afraid of heights?"

"I don't know! How can computers run the Internet? It's all a mystery to me!"

"Why didn't you tell Archie you were afraid of heights?"

"Archie installed me in the Larrymobile. How was I supposed to know that your car changed into an airplane?"

Larryboy dove low over the city.

"WHOOOOOOOOOOOAAA!" screamed Fred. "I'm going to be sick!"

"Twister dead ahead!" Larryboy shouted.

"Do you have to say the word *dead?* I can't look. I'm keeping my eyes closed."

"You're a computer. You don't have eyes."

The Larryplane closed in on the twister, which swirled just outside the city.

"My ears are popping!" shouted Fred. "My ears are popping!"

"You're a computer. You don't have ears."

The tornado appeared to be heading straight for a farmhouse. The Larryplane picked up speed.

"Remind me why we are about to fly into a tornado," Fred begged him, increasingly panicked.

"We're going to try to turn off this twister. But don't worry, Fred. Archie made some changes to the plane so it can survive two-hundred-mile-per-hour, twisting winds."

"But how do you know his changes will work? Archie isn't perfect! He made *me*, didn't he?"

Larryboy had to admit that Fred had a good point. But there was no turning back now. The Larryplane zoomed straight into the side of the monstrous storm, and the funnel cloud swallowed the little plane like a giant fly.

CHAPTER 11
A MOOOO-VING EXPERIENCE
2:55 P.M.

Larryboy couldn't believe it. He was looking at one of the greatest mysteries of nature—the inside of a tornado. The Larryplane spun around and around and around and around and around and around and...Now add about three hundred million more *arounds*, all in about ten minutes. That's how fast the twister spun the plane.

By this time, Fred had completely blacked out. (Of course, computers can't black out, but leave it to Fred to find a way.)

Inside the vortex of the tornado, all sorts of things whirled around, along with the Larryplane.

Pieces of wood.

A rocking chair.

Ma Mushroom riding a bicycle.

Two penguins playing checkers.

An air compressor.

A flying monkey.

An oil tanker.

And three cows.

At the state fair every year, Larryboy's

favorite ride was the Nauseator, which spun him at speeds that would tie his stomach in knots for days. But that was nothing compared to this twister.

Suddenly, the wind whipped the cockpit hatch off of the plane, leaving Larryboy completely exposed to the storm. He ducked as a piece of wood zipped by him, just inches above his head.

"That was close. Good thing I've got catlike reflexes. Otherwise, I might have—"

WHAP!

Larryboy forgot about the funnel effect—what goes around comes around. The piece of wood got him on the next lap around.

When Larryboy regained consciousness, he was lying in a haystack. His airplane was sticking through the side of a barn, and Fred was calling for a medic.

Very woozy and sore, Larryboy got up on his wobbly feet.

Feet?

Larryboy looked down. He not only had feet. He had *four* of them!

Running to a nearby farm pond, Larryboy stared at his reflection in the water. He couldn't believe what he saw.

HE WAS A COW!

How in the world did his brain wind up in the body of a cow? Was it all a bad dream? Was it from hitting his head? Had he landed somewhere over the rainbow?

Then somebody behind him said, **"MOOO."**

Larryboy whirled around and fell over. (It's not so easy to whirl on four feet.) He couldn't believe what he saw. He

saw himself wandering around nibbling on grass. Or at least he saw someone who *looked* just like him wandering around nibbling on grass.

Larryboy, the cow, ambled over to the other Larryboy. "Who are you?" he asked. "Are you me? Or am I you?"

The other Larryboy swallowed a mouthful of grass. Then he simply smacked his lips and said, **"MOOOOOO."**

This was unbelievable. Larryboy's brain had been switched with the brain of a cow!

CHAPTER 12

AN EMERGENCY WEATHER BULLETIN
3:29 P.M.

We interrupt this story with an emergency weather bulletin.

A cool-kid warning remains in effect for the rest of our book. These cool kids strike like lightning and pack heavy winds. Be ready to seek shelter at a moment's notice.

The National Weather Service has also issued a kindness watch, which means conditions are right for acts of kindness to occur. In fact, there is a thirty percent chance of lightly scattered kindness.

So keep your eyes open.

We now return you to your regularly scheduled story...

CHAPTER 13

BOWLED OVER

3:30 P.M.

It's amazing how quickly a fad can spread. By afternoon, a bunch of kids at Bumbly Park were strutting their stuff with clothes hangers in their shirts.

Meanwhile, Junior left the *Daily Bumble* and cut through the park on his bicycle. He spotted Ricky and Ziggy, who were loaded down with the afternoon edition of the newspaper.

"I'm here to help you deliver papers," Junior beamed. Hanging with Ziggy and Ricky brought with it amazing prestige. *Wait till my friends see this!* he thought.

"Great!" said Ziggy. "Maybe you can go bowling with us when we're done."

"Really? I'd love to!" he replied. But then it hit him. Ziggy wasn't talking about the kind of bowling most people do. Ziggy meant bully-bowling.

Junior's heart sank. "Ummm...I don't know if I can."

Ziggy's eyes became dark and narrowed. "Listen, Asparagus. You're one of us now. And that doesn't happen to many Veggies. You'd better go bowling with us...or else."

Being cool suddenly didn't seem all that hot. Junior gulped. "Who...who are you planning to bowl over?"

"Who else?" laughed Ziggy. "Those two losers over there."

Junior looked down the sidewalk. Ziggy was talking about Wally and Herbert, who were both loaded down with their own newspapers to deliver.

"But you've already bowled them over today."

"We're trying for a turkey...that means we've got two strikes to go!" said Ricky.

"We'll do the actual bowling. All you have to do is retrieve our bowling balls when we're done," Ziggy told him. "Whataya say, kid?"

This was Junior's big chance to take a stand. But which stand would he take? To be cool like Ziggy and Ricky? Or stand up for what's right and show kindness?

"We're waiting for an answer, Asparagus," growled Ziggy.

Junior didn't know what to do.

"Come on, Asparagus. Be cool and rule. Or be a loser and drool."

"Either way, you're part of the game," snickered Ziggy. "You can help us, or we're going to bowl *you* over. Take your pick."

Junior looked around. A group of kids had collected and were hanging on every word. He took one last look at Ziggy's ugly stare. He was scared.

"Let's go bowling," he muttered.

CHAPTER 14

COW-BOY
3:32 P.M.

Meanwhile, we last left Larryboy in the body of a cow, while Fred the Computer called for a medic.

"I'm melting, I'm melting!" shouted Fred.

Larryboy ran over to the crashed Larryplane, which was still sticking out of the side of the barn.

"Do something!" Fred said. "Call an ambulance! Call a programmer!"

"You're a computer, Fred. You don't need an ambulance."

"I've already lost two pints of data," said Fred, freaking out. "I'm going to need a transfusion from a laptop. Hurry! I'm moving toward the bright light!"

Suddenly, the computer went quiet for a few moments—very unusual for Fred. "Hey, you're not Larryboy. You're a talking cow," he said.

"No, I'm Larryboy. That twister put my brain in the body of a cow."

Stunned silence. Then Fred started giggling. Pretty soon, the computer couldn't control himself.

"Say, Larryboy, did you hear this one? What do you call it when super cows do battle? Steer Wars!"

Larryboy was not amused.

"And where does Superman's cow live? In Moo-tropolis!"

"Very funny, Fred."

"Hey, don't have a cow, man! Or should I say, don't have a man, cow?" Fred couldn't stop laughing.

While Fred continued with his antics, Larryboy used one of his hooves to push the communicator button in the plane's cockpit. Archie popped up on the high-definition video monitor.

"Larryboy, are you behind that cow?" asked Archie. "Larryboy! Come in! A cow seems to have triggered the videophone."

"Bad news, Archie. I *am* the cow. My brain is in this cow's body."

There was a long pause on the other end of the videophone. Archie blinked in shock. "Okay, don't panic. Don't panic. We can still do this."

"How?" asked Larryboy.

"How now brown cow?" snickered Fred.

"Listen closely," Archie ordered. "There's a spare pair of supersuction ears in the back of the Larryplane. I think they'll fit over the ears on your cow head."

"What do you call a hero who gets superpowers after being bitten by a radioactive cow?" asked Fred. "A moootant!"

"There's also a minicomputer under the front seat—a computer so small you can carry it like a portable CD player," said Archie. "Plug it into the airplane's controls and download Fred onto it. That way, you'll have Fred with you for help."

"What sound effect does Bat-Cow make when he fights villains?" giggled Fred. **"COW-POW!"**

"I'm not sure that I really want Fred with me."

"Of course you do. Without him, I don't see how you'd be able to track down Plum Loco. I'm convinced that he's behind all of this."

"But Fred is awfully emotional," said Larryboy. "One second he's getting mad. Then he's panicking. Now he can't stop laughing."

"I'm e-moooooo-tional," laughed Fred.

"I programmed emotions into Fred so that he'd be a computer with a heart. Remember your superhero lesson? Heroes have a heart. But perhaps I overdid the emotion programming."

"I'm e-mooooooooo-tional," Fred chuckled again.

"Oh dear," Larryboy sighed, but he did exactly as Archie asked. He slipped a pair of supersuction ears over his cow ears, downloaded Fred onto the minicomputer, and attached the computer to the cowbell hanging around his neck.

"Look at me! I'm a cowbell!" shouted Fred. "Of course, I'd rather be a cow-*boy*, but I suppose this will have to do."

As for Larryboy, he stood in the farm field with a purple mask on his face, supersuction plunger ears over his cow-ears, and a minicomputer around his neck.

The fate of Bumblyburg rested in the hands of a cow.

CHAPTER 15

BRAIN-TWISTER 2
3:44 P.M.

Larryboy had to
admit that Fred came in handy.
Within three minutes, Fred had figured
out that there was a secret headquarters
underground—right beneath their feet.

And a minute after that, Fred figured out that
you could enter the secret headquarters through the
farmhouse's storm-cellar doors.

And two minutes after *that*, he came up with the
password to get them inside the cellar.

And ten seconds after *that*...Larryboy tumbled head
over hooves down the cellar stairs.

"You're an *udder* failure when it comes to going
down stairs," chuckled Fred.

"I don't think I'll ever wish I had feet again," muttered Larryboy.

The first room they entered in the underground
headquarters was filled with pictures and diagrams of
brains. A giant, clear-plastic model of a brain stood in
the center of the room. But there was no sign of life.

The song, "Don't Go Breaking My Brain,"
played over an intercom.

"Hook me up to one of those computers

on the wall," said Fred.

"Sure thing."

One minute later, Fred was sifting through all of the information on Plum Loco's computer system.

"Archie is right," Fred calculated. "Plum Loco is the guy who's been switching brains around. His invention is called the Brain-Twister—a tornado that switches brains between different bodies. Amazing."

But suddenly, Fred started crying. It began with quiet weeping. But then he cut loose with some heavy sobs.

"Now what, Fred? You're a computer," Larryboy told him. "You can't cry."

"It's my disk drive, and I'll cry if I want to," sobbed Fred. "I've just tapped into Plum Loco's diary...and...and..."

"What is it, Fred?"

"It seems as though Plum Loco never had any friends growing up. Other kids teased him and called him a brainiac. Nerd. Geek. Four eyes. It's all so sad...I...I..."

"Get a hold of yourself, Fred."

"Plum Loco never received a single birthday present when he was growing up."

"Never?" asked Larryboy. "So that explains his dastardly deeds."

"Yes, it does. Plum Loco decided to use his massive brainpower to devise mean tricks. And get this. Today is his birthday, which probably explains the reason for his attack. It's all so sad..."

"Is Plum Loco the one who's been stealing all the stuffed animals?" asked Larryboy.

"That's right."

"But why?"

"It seems that Plum Loco surrounded himself with stuffed animals while he was growing up. Since no one was ever kind to him, he had to turn to stuffed animals, the next best thing. He could never get enough. They were warm. They were fuzzy. Since then, his plan has been to take every stuffed animal in the world."

Fred was boo-hooing now.

"Control yourself or you're going to blow your circuits," said Larryboy. "Besides, we've got to be quiet."

Larryboy crept silently into the next room—as quiet as one could with four cow hooves and a bell. He heard someone talking.

Peering out from behind a stack of gadgets and blinking contraptions, Larryboy spotted Plum Loco. The mad scientist was in the middle of the room, fiddling with the controls of a newer, larger Brain-Twister. The round ship hovered three feet above the ground.

"Switching brains with a superhero like Lemon Twist was so much fun," Plum Loco told his Teddy Bear. "But the citizens of Bumblyburg haven't seen anything yet. My first Brain-Twister was a toy compared to the Brain-Twister 2. I'll be able to switch the brains of *hundreds* of people all at the same time! And then I'll get my final revenge by destroying the entire city of Bumblyburg!"

"You'd better do something fast," Fred whispered to Larryboy. "Notice I said the word *you*."

Fred was right. It was time for this cow to become an action hero.

CHAPTER 16

THE BIG SWITCHEROO
4:04 P.M.

"Cowabunga, baby!" shouted Larryboy as he leaped out from his hiding place. He tried a "cow fu" stance, but that wasn't easy with four cow legs. Larryboy wound up flat on his tail.

Plum Loco spun around in surprise. Then he laughed, threw open the hatch on the top of the Brain-Twister 2, and hopped inside. "I'll get you, my pretty, and your little computer, too!" he cackled.

As the Brain-Twister 2 fired up its power, Larryboy turned his cow head and fired a supersuction plunger ear. The plunger tore across the room and stuck fast to the side of the ship. **THONK!**

"Now what?" asked Fred.

"I haven't thought that far ahead," said Larryboy.

"Big mistake."

Fred was right.

The Brain-Twister 2 rose high in the air until it hovered midway between the floor and the ceiling. And then it began to spin. Slowly at first. Then it built up speed and power.

Since Larryboy (and Fred) were connected to the ship

by the plunger cord, they, too, began to spin. Faster and faster and faster and faster.

"AHHҺHҺҺHҺҺHHHҺҺҺHҺҺHHHҺHҺҺHHHҺҺHҺ!" Larryboy yelled.
"AHHҺHҺҺHHҺHHHҺҺҺHҺҺHHHҺHҺҺHHHҺҺHҺ!" Fred yelled.

The Brain-Twister 2 began spinning at speeds that would make an astronaut sick to his stomach. As it twirled, the ship created a powerful, spinning wind. It had become a twister! Directly above the twister, the ground opened up. If anyone had been watching, it would have appeared as if the very earth itself had opened its mouth.

Come to think of it, there *was* someone watching above ground. The cow—actually the cow in Larryboy's body. Despite the fact that he was busy munching on grass, this spectacle caused even him to be curious. So this cow (who looked like Larryboy) wandered over to the big hole that had just opened up in the ground. He peered inside.

"MOOOOOO?"

The twister rose out of the ground. Within an instant, the tornado had sucked up the cow that looked like Larryboy along with every other chicken and pig that it passed over as it cut across the farmland.

Then as it turned and headed for the city, the tornado began hurling animals out of its funnel cloud—just as fast as it was sucking them up. It looked like it was raining pigs and chickens.

"OOF!"
"MOO!"
"OUCH!"
"OINK!"

That was the sound of Larryboy, Fred, the cow, and a

pig being spit out of the twister and hitting the ground. But the million-dollar question was, when they landed, who had whose brain?

The good news was that Larryboy's brain was no longer inside that cow. A pig's brain was inside the poor creature instead.

The bad news was that Larryboy's brain did not wind up back inside his own body. His brain ended up inside the portable minicomputer, where Fred had been stored.

Hmmmmmm…Then what happened to Fred the Computer?

His computer brain wound up inside Larryboy's body.

Fred looked down at his brand-new, cucumber body and said, "Larryboy, I don't think we're in Kansas anymore."

CHAPTER 17
CLOUDY, WITH A CHANCE OF KINDNESS
4:05 P.M.

Meanwhile, back at Bumbly Park, Ziggy and Ricky had bowled perfect strikes. Ziggy's bowling ball sent Wally hurtling into the bushes, while Ricky's hook shot knocked Herbert ten feet into the air. Their newspapers went flying in all directions.

Junior felt horrible as he watched Wally and Herbert struggle to get up and then run around trying to catch their papers before they blew away. Lots of other kids stood around watching, too. Only Laura Carrot had the courage—and the heart—to help them.

"Gee thanks, Laura," said Wally.

"Yeah, you're a pal," added Herbert. "What's gotten into Junior today?"

"He's too cool to care," muttered Laura, her anger rising.

Meanwhile, Ziggy and Ricky prepared for another frame of bully bowling.

"Who do you want to take out this time?" Ziggy asked Ricky.

"I'll take Wally *and* the carrot girl. It's a tricky shot, but I love a challenge."

"But you already got your turkey!" Junior exclaimed.

"Chill out, Asparagus. We've got a perfect game going. Can't stop now."

"Wait till they pick up all of their papers," Ricky snickered. "Then we'll roll again."

Junior didn't know what to say. He looked at all of the kids standing around, just watching. No one wanted to help. No one showed an ounce of kindness—except for Laura.

"This isn't who I want to be," Junior found himself saying. "I quit."

"You what?" asked Ricky.

"Don't have the guts to bowl with the big boys?" Ziggy smirked.

"This isn't my kind of game," Junior told them. "Someday you just might wind up in Wally and Herbert's shoes, and you won't like it either!"

"They don't *wear* shoes, Asparagus boy!" Ricky chuckled.

"Besides, that'll never happen," Ziggy told him. "There's no way we'd ever be caught wearing anything they would wear."

"And *I'm* no longer going to be caught wearing *this* silly thing in *my* clothes!" Junior said. Then he yanked the hanger out from under his shirt and rushed over to help his friends pick up their papers.

"Gee thanks, Junior," smiled Herbert.

"I'm sorry I didn't do this sooner," Junior told his friends.

"We're *all* going to be sorry any second now," said Laura. "We're about to be bowled over."

Ziggy and Ricky were lining up their next shots.

"I'm not afraid of them anymore," said Junior.

"Don't sweat it, guys," said Herbert. "It looks like we've got much bigger problems than Ziggy and Ricky."

Wally, Laura, and Junior looked in the direction that Herbert was staring. Rising high above the city was a storm. It was the biggest twister they had ever seen. Its black tail scoured the ground like a snake.

And the monster was heading their way.

CHAPTER 18

TWIST AND SHOUT
4:19 P.M.

Fred couldn't have been happier.

"Look at me! I'm a cucumber! I've got a body!" Fred said as he hopped around like a little kid on Christmas morning.

"That body is just on loan," scolded Larryboy. His brain was still trapped inside the minicomputer, which still dangled from the cow's neck.

"Let's do the twist!" Fred swiveled his hips, dancing like a crazed cucumber. "Let's do the—"

"Fred..."

"Look at me! I can stand on my head!"

"*Fred...*"

"Look at me! I can do the limbo!"

"FRED! We don't have time to waste. That twister is heading straight for the heart of Bumblyburg."

Fred finally stopped jumping around and caught his breath. "Sorry, Larryboy. I got carried away."

"The entire city of Bumblyburg is going to get carried away by powerful winds if we don't do something fast!"

"But what?" asked Fred. "I can't think straight in this body. I don't know how you do it. And how do you scratch an itch in the middle of your back? It's starting to drive me crazy."

Fred paced back and forth, itching and fidgeting.

"Come to think of it, these clothes make it hard to concentrate," complained Fred. "This spandex is so tight I can hardly breathe. How do you stand it?"

Larryboy's eyes lit up. "Did you say clothes? Fred, you're a genius!"

"Can't you wear Bermuda shorts or something that allows a little more freedom of movement?" Fred asked, not paying attention to Larryboy.

"Put on tender mercy and kindness as if they were your clothes," Larryboy said, remembering the words from the *Superhero Handbook*. "It's the secret weapon that will stop Plum Loco! But we'd better act fast."

"We should?"

"Yes!"

So they did.

CHAPTER 19

MIND GAMES
4:25 P.M.

The twister hurled through
Bumblyburg with a vengeance. It
tossed billboards through the air like
giant Frisbees. It tossed garbage cans
around like toys. The storm also sucked up
fleeing Veggies like…well, kind of like
Larryboy's Cyclone 1000 vacuum cleaner. And by
the time the twister dropped the Veggies back onto
the ground, their brains had been switched.

There was complete chaos in Bumblyburg.

Baby Lou Carrot's brain had been switched with a
policeman's.

Bob the Tomato's brain wound up in Vicki
Cucumber's head.

Junior Asparagus's brain had been switched with
Laura the Carrot's.

Most amazing of all…

Wally's and Herbert's brains had been switched
with Ziggy's and Ricky's. That's right. The storm
hit Bumbly Park with amazing speed, and it did
some bowling of its own. It bowled over Wally,

Herbert, Ziggy, and Ricky, and then spit them back out about ten seconds later.

Thunderstruck, Ziggy and Ricky looked down at their new bodies. Ziggy found himself wearing a Hawaiian shirt and silly sunglasses. Ricky was wearing a turtleneck sweater and a baseball cap that was on backwards.

"AHHHHHHHHHHHHHHHHHHHHHHHHHHHHHH!"

It was their worst nightmare.

"I want my mommy!" cried Ricky.

Meanwhile, the twister turned onto Bumbly Boulevard and set its target on downtown Bumblyburg. Plum Loco was ready for some serious revenge. He aimed to flatten every building he could find. And no one could stand in his way.

But someone *was* standing in his way. Two someones, in fact.

Larryboy and Fred.

CHAPTER 20

THE SECRET WEAPON
5:20 P.M.

Fred (still in Larryboy's body) and Larryboy (still stuck inside the minicomputer) held their ground. But it wasn't easy. Wind hit them like invisible linebackers. The tornado bore down on them, growling and rumbling and spitting lightning.

But Fred and Larryboy wouldn't budge. They stood right beside the Larryplane, which they had been surprised to find still working. Fred had flown it to the rescue by remote control.

"Is it time to use our secret weapon?" Fred asked.

"It's time."

Larryboy and Fred began to sing as loudly as they could. Their voices boomed from the speaker system built into the Larryplane.

"HAPPY BIRTHDAY TO YOU! HAPPY BIRTHDAY TO YOU! HAPPY BIRTHDAY DEAR LOCO! HAPPY BIRTHDAY TO YOUUUUUUUU!"

The twister slowed down—but just barely. Larryboy and Fred continued to belt out their song, again and again.

By the time they

sang "Happy Birthday" for the fourth time, the tornado had come to a complete stop—only a short distance from our heroes. A mechanical arm shot out of the funnel cloud with a chair at the end of it. And sitting in the chair was none other than Plum Loco.

Plum Loco looked confused.

"How...how did you know that today is my birthday?" he stammered.

"I'm a computer," said Fred. "It's my job to know those things.

"Show him what we've got," said Larryboy.

Smiling, Fred reached into the cockpit of the Larryplane. He pulled out three brightly wrapped birthday presents and a delicious chocolate cake.

"For me?" gasped Plum Loco.

"Happy birthday, Loco!"

The mad scientist was stunned. No one had ever been so kind to him.

"We're sorry you never got any presents when you were growing up," said Larryboy.

"What a bummer," added Fred. "So happy birthday!"

"How did you know that I never got any presents when I was growing up?" asked the plum.

"Like I said, I'm a computer," said Fred. "It's my job to know these things."

Plum Loco had unplugged his emotions a long time ago. But somehow, some way, these three presents, the birthday cake, and the song triggered something buried deep inside him. They triggered a tiny spark of kindness.

Why else would Plum Loco do what he did next?

"I tell you what, guys," he said. "Since you scratched my back, I'll scratch yours."

"Good!" beamed Fred. "I was wondering how I was going to get that itch scratched!"

"No, I think he means he's going to do something kind for us, since we are being kind to him," pointed out Larryboy.

"What about my itch?"

"I'm going to put your brains back where they were," Plum Loco said as he pushed a button on a remote control. A tiny tornado shot from the side of the large twister and whirled straight toward Fred and Larryboy. It spun them around for a minute and then put them safely on the ground.

Their brains were back where they belonged.

"There's no place like home," said Larryboy, looking down at his cucumber body. It felt good to be back home in his very own body.

Fred didn't even mind being put back inside the mini-computer until he could be returned to his regular home. Bodies can be a lot of trouble, he decided.

"Thanks, Plummy," said Larryboy. "But can I ask one more thing?"

"Fire away, Larryboy," said the plum as he busily unwrapped the first present. It was a new lab coat, specially made for him by the Super Seamstresses at the costume factory.

"Can you turn off this twister...please? Someone could get hurt."

Plum Loco looked up sharply. Had Larryboy asked too much? Was Plum Loco's moment of kindness over?

A smile broke out on the plum's face. "Let it be my way of saying thanks."

Unfortunately, there was one big problem. Before Plum Loco could make a move to turn off the twister, the torna-do began to inch forward—without anyone steering it.

"Watch out behind you!" Larryboy warned.

"Uh-oh," said Plum Loco. "This twister is too powerful for my old braking system. It's about to—"

All at once, the twister hurled Plum Loco out of his chair and took off like a runaway train. The twister was once again headed straight for downtown Bumblyburg.

CHAPTER 21

THE IMPERFECT STORM
5:44 P.M.

Larryboy leaped into the cockpit of the Larryplane as Plum Loco stared bug-eyed at his out-of-control creation.

"Larryboy, let me go with you!" the plum shouted. "I'm the only one who knows how to turn it off!"

"Hop in, Plummy!"

The Larryplane may have been battle-bruised from the previous twister, but it could still outrun the tornado. As it raced alongside the giant twister, Larryboy fired a supersuction plunger from one of the wings.

THONK!

The plunger hit home. It zipped through the dark funnel cloud and struck the core—the heart of the twister that spun the storm. But once connected to the Brain-Twister, the Larryplane began to spin around and around and around.

"Here we go again!" shouted Fred.

"How do I turn the twister off?" Larryboy yelled over the roar.

"You have to get inside," answered Plum Loco. "Then push the red button!"

"Roger that!" Then Larryboy attempted

the impossible. As the plane spun around and around, he hooked himself onto the tether line, which extended from the plane to the center of the twister. He was going to slide down the cord and into the middle of the twister.

"Watch out for the wood this time!" Fred called out.

He was right. Pieces of wood spun around and around the funnel cloud. Larryboy had to dodge them all if he wanted to pull this off.

ZIPPPPPPPP!

Hooked to the tether, Larryboy slid down the zip line. "Oops."

Oops was right. Just as our hero was heading for the side of the tornado, about six chunks of wood came flying around the side of the cloud.

One piece of wood skimmed his head. Two raced right by his back. One grazed his stomach. So he hopped on top of the fifth and rode it like a splintered surfboard.

"I DID IT!" Larryboy shouted before Fred could shout... **"WATCH OUT!"**

Larryboy fired a supersuction ear just in time, deflecting the wood right before it slammed into his face.

Meanwhile, the tornado was closing in on the first building in its path—the Burger Bell restaurant.

The wild wind shredded two telephone poles.

Dirt spiraled into the air, blinding Larryboy.

The caped cucumber disappeared through the side of the funnel cloud.

Pieces of the Burger Bell's roof began to peel off the restaurant.

Deep inside the twister, Larryboy made his way into Plum Loco's ship.

The twister bounced a car on the ground like a basketball.

Ma Mushroom was again peddling her bike in midair.

Larryboy found the red button and pushed it.

Suddenly, the twister came to a halt. It burbled and gurgled and began to come apart. The black cloud rolled and churned…

And then it exploded. **POP! POOF!**

The tornado burst apart into millions of little, black puffy clouds.

The Larryplane was hurled backwards by the blast. It spun out of control, nose-diving toward Earth.

Fred's life flashed in front of his circuits.

Larryboy was nowhere to be seen.

CHAPTER 22

AN EMERGENCY WEATHER BULLETIN
6:06 P.M.

We interrupt the climax of this story with an emergency weather bulletin.

The National Weather Service has cancelled the Cool-Kid Warning. The storm has passed and the all-clear has sounded. Expect showers of kindness through the rest of the day.

We now return you to your regularly scheduled conclusion ...

CHAPTER 23

THE GREATEST DAY
THE NEXT DAY...

When Larryboy came to, he was in a hospital bed with a bandage on his head. He was surrounded by friendly faces—Bob the Tomato, Vicki, Archie, Lemon Twist, Bok Choy, Laura, Junior, Wally, and Herbert.

Larryboy looked around at his friends. He was groggy, but smiling.

"I had the strangest dream," Larryboy said. "And you were in it, Bob. And you were in it, Archie. And you too, Bok Choy."

"It wasn't a dream," Archie explained. "It really happened. You got quite a bump on your head."

"But you'll be glad to know that the twister has been destroyed," Laura smiled.

"When you pushed the button, it exploded," added Bob.

"And when the tornado blew up, everyone's brains were returned to them. Everybody's back to normal," said Bok Choy.

"Well, almost everybody," Junior pointed out. "Ricky and Ziggy have apologized to

Wally and Herbert. That's not exactly normal."

"And Fred...what happened to Fred?" asked Larryboy.

"I'm right here, good buddy!"

Larryboy turned his head to the left. There, lying in the hospital bed next to him, was the computer. An IV ran from the hospital's computer into Fred's side.

"The storm is over?" Larryboy asked.

"That's right," said Bob. "The sun is shining. It's a new day."

"But what about Plum Loco?" asked Larryboy. "Is he okay?"

"Just take a look to your right," said Lemon Twist.

Larryboy turned his head to the other side. There, in another hospital bed, lay the mad scientist—only he wasn't so mad anymore.

"Hello, Larryboy," said Plum Loco. "I'm sorry I switched everyone's brains, robbed the toy store, uprooted trees, and tried to destroy the city."

"You're forgiven," said Larryboy.

All at once, the door of the hospital room was flung open.

"I got here as quickly as I could, doncha know!" It was Officer Olaf. He was all smiles. He was lugging a huge load of gifts for Plum Loco, Larryboy, and Fred the Computer.

Officer Olaf pulled out a box of chocolates and handed them to Plum Loco—a box shaped like a brain. "Just the way you like it."

Right behind Olaf came Dr. Nezzer, with a big grin on his face and waving a set of X-rays. "Great news, Mr. Loco!" the doctor exclaimed. "Your X-rays are back! And they show, without a doubt, that in addition to having a great big brain, you do have a heart!"

"Thanks everyone," Plum Loco said as he looked around the room. "You're all being so kind, and I really don't deserve it."

"Nonsense!" said Bok Choy, as he stepped from behind a curtain. He pushed out a cart, which carried the largest cake any of them had ever seen.

"I think Larryboy and Fred were in the middle of celebrating someone's birthday yesterday, right before the tornado spun out of control," said Bok Choy. "There's no reason we can't finish the celebration."

So the entire group broke out into song.

"HAPPY BIRTHDAY TO YOU! HAPPY BIRTHDAY TO YOU! HAPPY BIRTHDAY DEAR LOCO! HAPPY BIRTHDAY TO YOU!"

Plum Loco leaned forward and blew out the candles.

"What did you wish for?" asked Laura.

"I didn't need to make a wish," smiled the plum, looking around. "I've already gotten what I've always wanted."

"Let's eat!" shouted Fred. "I'm starving! I want the biggest piece!"

"You can't eat cake," said Larryboy. "You're a computer."

"Then pass the computer chips."

So the party began. This really was the greatest day in Plum Loco's life. But I suppose you already figured that out.

After all, that's what you call a no-brainer.

THE END

Larryboy and the Yodelnapper
Softcover 0-310-70562-2

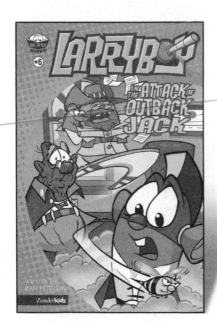

Larryboy in the Attack of Outback Jack
Softcover 0-310-70649-1

Larryboy in the Good, the Bad, and the Eggly
Softcover 0-310-70650-5

ALSO AVAILABLE ON VHS
MORE LARRYBOY ADVENTURES
AT A STORE NEAR YOU!

Larryboy and the Angry Eyebrows
(Episode 1) VHS

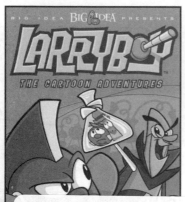

...delnapper
...HS